For Joe

First published 1995 by Walker Books Ltd
87 Vauxhall Walk, London SE11 5HJ

This edition published 2003

10 9 8 7 6 5 4 3 2 1

© 1995 Anita Jeram

This book has been typeset in Columbus

Printed in Hong Kong

British Library Cataloguing in Publication Data:
a catalogue record for this book is
available from the British Library

ISBN 0-7445-9244-5

Contrary Mary

Anita Jeram

WALKER BOOKS
AND SUBSIDIARIES
LONDON • BOSTON • SYDNEY

When Mary got up this morning she was feeling contrary. She put her cap on back to front and her shoes on the wrong feet.

"Are you awake, Mary?"
her mum called.
"No!" said Contrary Mary.

For breakfast there
was hot toast with
peanut butter.
"What would you like,
Mary?" asked Mum.
"Roast potatoes and gravy,
please," said Contrary Mary.

When they went
to the shops,
it was raining.

"Come under
the umbrella, Mary,"
said Mum.
But Contrary Mary
didn't. She just danced
about, getting wet.

All day long,
Contrary Mary did
contrary things.
She rode her

bicycle backwards.
She went for
a walk
on her hands.

She read a book upside
down. She flew her
kite along the ground.
Mary's mum shook her head.
"Mary, Mary, quite
contrary," she said.
And then she
had an idea.

That evening,
at bedtime, instead of tucking
Mary in the right way round,
Mary's mum tucked her in
upside down.

Then she opened
the curtains,
turned on the
light, kissed Mary's
toes and said,

"Good Morning!"

Mary laughed and laughed.
"Contrary Mum!"
she said.

"Do you love me, Contrary
Mary?" asked Mary's mum,
giving her
a cuddle.

"No!" said Contrary Mary. And she gave her mum a great big kiss.